8-7

5.00

Max and the Very Rare Bird

by Graham Percy

THE CHILD'S WORLD
Mankato, Minnesota

For Martin

Illustrations and text copyright © 1991 by Graham Percy

First published in the United States of America
and Canada in 1991 by:

The Child's World
123 South Broad Street, Mankato, MN 56001

Designed by Lisa Tai

ISBN 0-89565-786-4

Library of Congress Cataloging-in-
Publication data is available

10 9 8 7 6 5 4 3 2 1

Printed and bound in Belgium by Proost, Turnhout

"This," said Grandpa, holding up an enormous old book he
was reading, "is the Little crested bottle-jar – a very rare
bird indeed. Grandma thinks she saw one down by the lake!"

"First thing tomorrow morning, I think we should all go on an expedition and see if we can spot one." "Oh yes Grandpa, that would be great." said Max and Meg together.

The next morning they all had a very early breakfast. Max and Meg each had six pieces of toast with honey. Max said it would save them carrying a lot of food on the expedition.

Outside on the porch, Grandpa had arranged what they would need. Grandpa and Grandma took the heavy things, Meg carried the telescope and Max carried the camera.

"Because of the fog you must remember to keep holding hands," Grandpa called back to Max and Meg. "Oh and Max, if we see that rare bird *don't* forget to take a picture."

At the bottom of the yard there was a maze. Suddenly a
pair of squirrels leapt out of a tree past Max's ear and ran
into the maze. Max laughed and chased after them.

The rest of the party had now reached the lake and started
looking at all the birds there. Grandpa wrote in his notebook
and Meg started to make a drawing of a beautiful swan.

Grandma thought she would take a picture of the sunrise
and turned to Max for the camera . . . but where was Max?
They all called out ''M-a-a-a-x'' but there was no reply.

Just then, on the other side of the lake, they saw their good friend, Mr. Potter, preparing his hot-air balloon for an early morning flight. Grandpa called out to him.

"Mr. Potter, can you help us? We've lost our Max." "Yes of course, come over at once," called back Mr. Potter. "We can all go up in my balloon and look for him."

So they rushed around the edge of the lake – through the reeds and the sloshy mud – and, when they reached the basket of Mr. Potter's balloon, they all piled in.

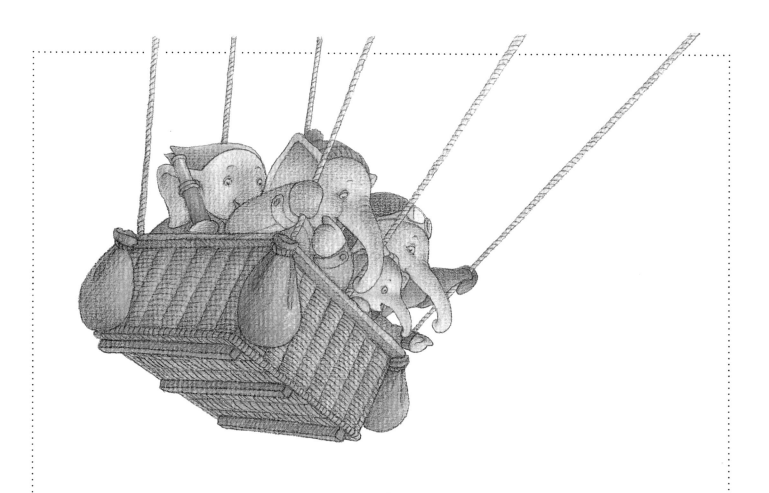

It was very crowded, but up they went and soon they were floating above the lake towards the house and the maze at the bottom of the yard. Suddenly Meg squealed, ''There he is!''

Sure enough, it was Max – right in the middle of the maze and waving up to them. Mr. Potter brought the balloon a little lower and then rolled a rope ladder down to him.

Max was just going to climb the rope ladder when Mr.
Potter saw that they were about to bump into a big oak tree.
"Hold on tight," he shouted to Max, "we're going up fast."

Just then Max felt something land on the rung above his head. He looked up to see . . . the Little crested bottle-jar. It was obviously enjoying the ride.

He called out to the others but they were noisily tumbling
around in the basket and couldn't hear him. So he reached
for the camera and . . . click . . . took a picture.

Now the balloon was rushing down towards the lawn beside their house. The little bird was a bit frightened by all this and swished off the ladder and away into the trees.

Bump! The balloon was down and everyone was chattering
at once but they all stopped when Max proudly announced,
''*I've* taken a picture of the Little crested bottle-jar.''

Now they all started to talk at once again. But above the din Mr. Potter cried out, "Bring that camera and the film, Max . . . you too Meg . . . we're going to the newspaper office."

Sure enough, that night when the evening newspaper was
delivered, there on the front page was a big picture of Max
and Meg holding the famous photograph.

Grandpa poked the fire then, turning to Max, said rather grumpily ''Young fellow, in the fog this morning you forgot to hold hands with your sister . . .''

But Grandma interrupted him, "Don't be too hard on him dear," she smiled, "after all, when Max saw that little bird on the rope ladder he *did* remember to take the picture!"